Be My Friend, Floppy Puppy

by Ann Tobias

illustrations by
Dubravka
Kolanovic

In Floppy Puppy's toy box there was a train, a set of blocks, and a round red ball. But all Floppy Puppy wanted was a friend.

So one day he took a book, his ball, and his set of blocks outside to look for someone to play with.

He saw birds flying to the feeder. "Are the seeds tasty?" asked Floppy Puppy, trying to start a friendly conversation, but the birds didn't hear him.

Floppy Puppy was
playing kick-the-ball
by himself when a
squirrel rushed past.

"Would you like to throw
the ball with me?" invited
the puppy, but the squirrel
didn't stop.

A field mouse crept by.

Floppy Puppy said, "Do you want to make a castle out of blocks?" But the mouse disappeared into a pile of bright leaves.

"Meow!"
Floppy Puppy looked up.

There, in the branches of a
tree, was a small orange kitten.

"Can you help me? I can't
get down," said Small Kitten.

Floppy Puppy knew just what to do!
Step by step Small Kitten made her way down.

"Thank you. Could we
make a castle with these
blocks?" she asked.